ALIEN INVADERS

MAX SILVER

HYDRONIX
DESTROYER OF THE DEEP

RED FOX

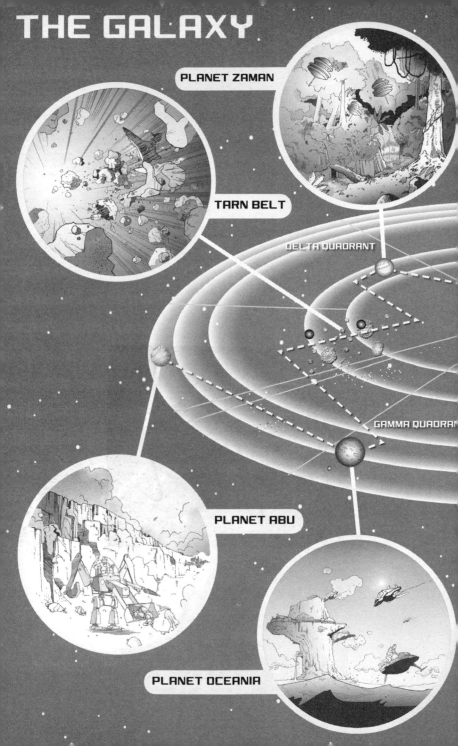

DOOM VORTEX

MOON OF GARR

ALPHA QUADRANT

PLANET MINGUS

GALACTIC CORE

PLANET EARTH

BETA QUADRANT

_ _ _ _ Cosmo's route

ATTENTION, ALL EARTHLINGS!

MY NAME IS G1 AND I AM CHIEF OF THE GALAXY'S SECURITY FORCE, G-WATCH. I BRING YOU GRAVE NEWS.

IT IS THE YEAR 2121, AND OUR PLANETS ARE UNDER ATTACK FROM THE OUTLAW KAOS. HE IS BEAMING FIVE ALIEN INVADERS INTO THE GALAXY, COMMANDING THEM TO DESTROY IT. IF THEY SUCCEED, THIS WILL BE THE END OF US ALL.

A HERO MUST BE FOUND TO SAVE US: ONE WHO WILL VENTURE THROUGH THE TREACHEROUS REGIONS OF SPACE; ONE WITH AN UNCOMMON COURAGE WITH WHICH TO FIGHT THESE INVADERS; ONE WHO POSSESSES THE POWER OF THE UNIVERSE! THAT HERO IS AN EARTHLING BOY. HE IS OUR ONLY HOPE.

INVADER ALERT!

"Mum, please can I have a go on the robo-bungee?" Jako asked.

Jako's mother was sunbathing in front of the beach hotel, tanning her yellow Utraxian skin. She opened her three eyes and smiled at him. "Of course you can."

"Brilliant!" Jako raced away, his tail swishing along the red sand. *Robo-bungee, here I come!*

Jako and his mother were holidaying

on Oceania, a water planet with nineteen artificial islands, a sparkling golden ocean and coral reefs. He ran down the beach, weaving between holidaymakers – more were out snorkelling, turbo-sailing and propeller-boarding. He stopped beside a thirty-metre-tall robot. Its huge metal hand was bouncing a frog-headed Mervish boy up and down into the water on an elastic bungee rope.

"Me next, please!" Jako called up.

The robo-bungee placed the grinning wet Mervish boy on the sand, then lifted Jako high into the air until he could see brightly coloured corals, shoals of fish – even some jumbola whales.

"Bungee attaching," the robot said, clamping the bungee rope around Jako's ankles. "*Ten . . . nine . . . eight . . .*"

Here I go! Jako thought excitedly. But just as he was readying himself to dive, he heard a sound like thunder and saw something hurtling down through the mauve sky. It hit the water about a mile away, sending up a plume of spray. A large dark shape moved towards the island.

"... *three*... *two* ... *one* ... *Bungee!*"

The robot sent Jako diving headfirst. As he plunged into the water, he glimpsed fish and corals and—

Jako gasped. Swimming towards the island was a terrifying alien with a barnacled face and enormous grasping tentacles! Suddenly the bungee rope pinged him back up into the air. He called out in panic: "There's a monster down there!"

Jako's stomach lurched as he dived into the water again. This time he saw the alien's huge tentacles curling around the island's flotation cylinders, trying to rip them free. He felt the bungee rope tighten, and it shot him back up. The whole island was rocking, the robo-bungee swinging him sideways with it.

"Help!" Jako called out. "There's a monster attacking the island!"

The hotel began to sway. Holidaymakers were screaming.

"Mum, help!" Jako called, bouncing helplessly up and down on the rope. He watched in terror as a tentacle reached

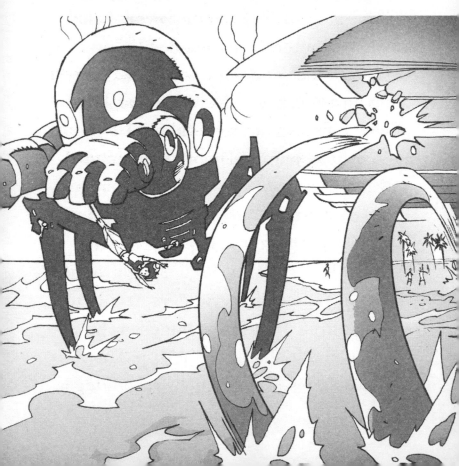

up out of the water and smashed a hole through the wall of the hotel. Another slammed down onto the beach, opening up a wide crack.

"The island's breaking up!" someone shouted. "Everyone off!"

"Robo-bungee, I want to get down!" Jako cried.

One of the alien's tentacles whacked the robo-bungee, toppling it into the ocean with Jako still attached. He gasped as he was pulled under the water, the weight of the sinking metal robot tugging on the bungee rope. He plummeted past the terrifying tentacled alien and heard it bellow: "I am Hydronix and, by order of Kaos, I have come to DESTROY!"

CHAPTER ONE

DESTINATION: OCEANIA

Cosmo heard a computerized voice speaking in his ear: "*Sleep acceleration complete. On the count of three, open your eyes. One . . . two . . . three . . .*"

He opened his eyes, feeling bright and alert. He was lying on the rest bunk in the cockpit of the Dragster 7000, wearing a sleep-acceleration headset. His co-pilot, Agent Nuri, a blue-skinned girl from the planet Etrusia, was at the controls.

"How long was I asleep for?" he asked.

"Only ten Earth minutes," Nuri replied.

"That's amazing! I feel like I've been asleep for hours."

"The sleep accelerator provides one hour's sleep for every minute. It works on your central nervous system. It should have replenished your energy for the battle ahead."

I could do with a sleep accelerator back on Earth when I'm too tired to get up for school, Cosmo thought with a grin.

Cosmo Santos was an eleven-year-old

Earthling boy on a mission for the galaxy's security force, G-Watch, to save the galaxy from five alien invaders. They were being beamed in by the galactic outlaw Kaos, using navicom transporter devices. So far Cosmo had defeated three of them: Rockhead, the living mountain; Infernox, the firestarter; and Zillah, the fanged predator. Now he was heading for the holiday planet Oceania to face the fourth invader, the underwater alien, Hydronix.

"How long until we're due to arrive, Nuri?" he asked, lifting off the headset.

"About eight minutes," Nuri replied. "Take the controls again while I check the kit."

Cosmo jumped into the pilot's seat. It was good to be back at the controls. The Dragster was leaving the galaxy's Great Western Tradeway, heading south. He tapped the spacescreen, activating its star plotter, and words lit up on the glass:

The spacescreen turned a bright flaming green as the Dragster flew through the trail of a comet. Cosmo turned the steering column and accelerated out of it, heading south towards Grekkox-2.

"Nuri, have you ever been to Oceania before?" he asked, tapping the spacescreen to deactivate the plotter.

"I once spent a week there, reef diving off Zeta Island," she replied from the back of the cockpit. "The ocean's an incredible golden colour and the corals are amazing."

Cosmo loved scuba diving. His dad, who'd been a G-Watch agent himself, had taught him one summer holiday back on Earth.

From the Dragster's control desk, the ship's bug-like brainbot, Brain-E, bleeped. "On Oceania there are nineteen holiday islands and all kinds of activities to enjoy: scuba diving, submarine rides, robo-bungee, propeller-boarding—"

"Brain-E, I don't think this mission is going to be a holiday for us," Nuri laughed. "We're going there to fight an alien invader, remember."

The brainbot flashed its lights nervously.

"Don't worry, I'll look after you," Cosmo told it kindly.

Cosmo had been recruited to G-Watch because of a power he possessed inside – the power of the universe – which was present in all living things, but uniquely strong in him. It gave him courage and a superhuman energy within.

The Dragster flew into Grekkox-2, and Cosmo saw a huge golden planet orbiting a red star. He recognized it from galacto-vision holiday commercials he'd seen back on Earth. "Oceania is straight ahead, Nuri," he said. "Prepare for entry."

Nuri jumped back into the co-pilot's seat and buckled up.

As Cosmo approached Oceania, he summoned his power, and his spacesuit started to glow. It was the Quantum Mutation Suit, G-Watch's most advanced piece of technology: living body armour infused with particles from the beginning of the universe. Activated by the power inside Cosmo, it could transform him into different alien forms.

The Dragster shook as it cut through Planet Oceania's atmosphere into a beautiful mauve sky. They flew down through wispy clouds until, far below, Cosmo saw the ocean. It stretched out in all directions, glittering in the sunlight.

"Wow!" he said. "The ocean really *is* golden here."

"There are microscopic gold-coloured plankton that live in the water," Nuri explained. "They're what the corals and the sea life feed on."

Cosmo could make out brightly coloured reefs: red, yellow and electric-blue. He saw shoals of alien fish swimming among them, and huge green whales spouting water.

"Look at the size of those whales!" he said.

Brain-E extended its stalk eyes, peering down through the spacescreen. "They're jumbola whales, Master Cosmo, a protected species."

Nuri checked the navigation console. "Keep your eyes peeled, team. According to G-Watch's scanners, Hydronix will have struck somewhere around here."

Cosmo looked out for signs of the invader. "Brain-E, what do we know about this alien?" he asked.

"My databank states that Hydronix originates from the Whirlpools of Vahl in the Doom Vortex. He is a barnacled alien of the deep, with enormous tentacles that are strong enough to crush rock."

Cosmo gulped. *That's all I need!*

"Look – there are the islands," Nuri said.

Cosmo flew over the first and second islands, looking down at holidaymakers on the beaches and in the water. But as the Dragster neared the third, he realized something was wrong. Spaceships were taking off, whizzing up into the sky. "Everyone's leaving," he said. Pieces of broken island were jutting from the ocean like icebergs. People were frantically swimming out to boats.

Cosmo slowed the Dragster and circled overhead. The island had split into chunks, with a hotel on one and sections of beach on the others. Its flotation cylinders were deflating, bubbling in the water, and the chunks were slowly sinking.

"Hydronix must have struck here!" Cosmo said, alarmed.

There was no one left on the broken island apart from one yellow-skinned Utraxian woman clinging to a palm tree on the sloping beach. She waved her arms hysterically, calling out.

"If the island sinks, that woman will

be sucked down with it!" Nuri said.

"We have to rescue her," Cosmo replied. He checked the planet's environment:

PLENTIFUL OXYGEN ... TEMPERATURE TWENTY-NINE DEGREES CENTIGRADE ... GRAVITY NORMAL.

The Dragster was now hovering directly above the woman. "Nuri, take the controls," he said.

Nuri took over and Cosmo headed for the kit shelves at the back of the cockpit. "What are you going to do?" she asked.

Cosmo slipped a harness over his body, then attached it to the Dragster's winch cable. "I'm going down to get her."

CHAPTER TWO

UNDERWATER RESCUE

Cosmo pressed the Dragster's exit release button, opening the cockpit door. A cool ocean breeze blew on his face and he leaned out, calling down to the Utraxian woman, "The island's sinking. You have to get off!"

"But my son Jako's down there somewhere!" She pointed into the water.

There was a loud groaning sound as the whole beach tipped vertically, nearly sending her into the ocean.

Cosmo grabbed the winch cable and stepped onto the footplate outside. "Nuri, hold the ship steady and lower me down," he said.

Nuri engaged the winch motor, and the long cable began unwinding, lowering Cosmo until he was level with the Utraxian woman. "You can't stay here or you'll drown," he said to her.

"But my son—"

Cosmo quickly removed his harness and slipped it over her head. "I'll find your son," he told her, and he called up to Nuri: "Winch her up."

As the woman rose into the air, Cosmo saw the water frothing around him. There was a hissing sound too. The island's flotation cylinders were emptying. Soon there would be nothing to keep it afloat.

"Now you, Cosmo!" Nuri called, lowering the empty harness back down, the woman safely aboard.

"No, Nuri. I have to save her son!" Cosmo shouted back. He shut his visor so that his helmet was full of air.

"You can't, Cosmo — it's too dangerous!"

But Cosmo ignored Nuri's warning, and the water rose up around him as the island started to sink.

He gripped the palm tree and plunged under the ocean with the sinking chunk of island. The water roared around his helmet as he dropped down and down. With a muffled *boom!* the chunk of island crunched onto the ocean floor, and a cloud of sand swirled up around him.

Cosmo breathed slowly and steadily. He had only a small amount of air in his helmet, and it wouldn't last long. As the sand cloud settled, he saw another chunk of island lying buckled and cracked on the bottom of the ocean, along with an enormous metal robot – a robo-bungee. And a yellow-skinned boy was trapped beneath it!

Cosmo swam towards him. The boy was tangled in a bungee rope, his arm trapped under the giant robot's steel hand. Around him lay sunken propeller-boards and scuba-diving equipment. To keep himself alive, the boy was gulping air from a split scuba tank.

"I'm going to help you!" Cosmo called.

He dug his spaceboots into the sand and grabbed the robot's thumb with both hands. He heaved as hard as he could, trying to lift its huge metal hand to free the boy, but it wouldn't budge.

Cosmo's breathing quickened from the exertion; the oxygen in his helmet was running out. He tried again, but still the metal hand wouldn't budge.

The boy shook his head, jerking his chin upwards in distress. Cosmo looked up and saw the island's hotel leaning on its side in the water, flotation cylinders bursting all around it.

Uh-oh, Cosmo thought. *In a few seconds it will sink and we'll be crushed!* He summoned his energy, then heaved again, but the robot was too heavy.

Suddenly, as if from nowhere, a group of ghostly fish-tailed aliens came swimming through the murky water towards him. They surrounded the robot and started to help, lifting its metal hand. The hand rose and the boy struggled out from beneath it.

Cosmo turned to thank them, but as quickly as they had appeared, the ghostly aliens swam off again, vanishing in the murky water. *Who were they?* he wondered. There was no time to find out. He glanced up and saw the hotel coming down through the water – heading straight for him! Quickly he untangled the boy from the bungee rope and pulled him free. "Swim!" he mouthed.

But the boy's arm was injured and hanging limply by his side. Cosmo pulled him along, kicking as hard as he could, and with a muffled *boom* the huge hotel building crashed down just behind them. Sand swirled in the water and Cosmo kicked his legs, swimming upwards, dragging the boy to safety. They broke the surface, and the boy gasped for air.

"Th-thank you. You saved my life," he said.

Cosmo flipped up his visor and took a deep breath. "No problem," he replied, relieved that the boy was safe.

He heard thrusters overhead. The Dragster was descending, its floats inflated, ready for landing on water.

The boy's mother called down from the open cockpit door: "Jako, you're alive!"

"I'm OK, Mum," the boy called back. "Thanks to him." He looked to Cosmo, smiling.

The Dragster touched down on the water and Cosmo swam over, pulling Jako along with him. Nuri helped the boy aboard and his mum swept him up in a hug.

"Thank you so much for saving him," she said to Cosmo.

Cosmo climbed aboard. "I had some help," he said, thinking of the strange underwater aliens that had helped him lift the robo-bungee's heavy metal hand. "Nuri, you'd better check his arm. It's injured."

Nuri sat Jako in her co-pilot's seat and gently felt along his arm. "It's fractured," she said. "Hold still a moment." She fetched a copper band from the Dragster's first-aid cabinet and clipped it around the boy's arm. It began to vibrate.

"What's this?" the boy asked, feeling it gently.

"It's a sonic ossifier," Nuri explained. "Keep it on for twenty minutes while it re-knits the bone."

Cosmo knelt beside the boy. "Your name's Jako, isn't it?"

"That's right," the boy replied.

"I'm Cosmo, and this is Agent Nuri. We're from G-Watch."

"G-Watch! Wow!" Jako said excitedly.

"Did you see what happened to the island?" Cosmo asked.

Jako nodded. "A monster did it! It had enormous tentacles, and it tore the island apart, bellowing that someone called Kaos had sent it here."

"Did you see which way it went?"

"After it attacked, I saw it swim away underwater towards Calzador."

"What's Calzador?" Cosmo asked.

"It's supposed to be beautiful," Jako said. "The hotel runs submarine tours there."

"We were planning to go sightseeing there later," his mother added.

Brain-E bleeped from the control desk. "Master Cosmo, Calzador is an underwater coral city famous for its beauty."

"Well, no one's going to do any sightseeing today," Cosmo said. He glanced out at the debris and rescue boats in the water, then up at the spaceships above, evacuating holidaymakers from Oceania.

When those holidaymakers arrive back on their planets, news of what's happened here will quickly spread, he thought. *The whole galaxy will soon fear Kaos.*

Nuri summoned a rescue boat to take Jako and his mother away. "It's time you two got to safety," she told them.

"What about you? What are you going to do?" Jako asked Cosmo.

"We're going after the invader," Cosmo replied. "We have to stop it. Come on, Nuri. It's time for a deep-sea dive."

CHAPTER THREE

THE WAY TO CALZADOR

Cosmo and Nuri stood at the Dragster's open door, preparing themselves. They each swallowed an oxygen pill so that they could breathe underwater. Cosmo felt the pill fizz on his tongue as the oxygen was released into his body. Then they attached torpedo fins to their spaceboots: large flippers fitted with turbo boosters to help them power through the water. Nuri fastened a waterproof compass onto her

utility belt for navigation, then screwed
a propeller attachment onto Brain-E.

Brain-E bleeped nervously. "Are you
sure you want me to come too?" it asked.

"We're a team, Brain-E," Nuri replied.
"We may need you."

"I'll protect you, Brain-E," Cosmo said.
"Come on, let's go find this alien." He
closed the visor of his Quantum
Mutation Suit and dived into the sea.

The water was clearing as the island debris settled on the sandy ocean floor. Below him, Cosmo could see patches of coral and colourful sea plants. He kicked his feet, engaging his torpedo fins, and headed downwards. He glanced back and saw Nuri swimming after him, with Brain-E beside her.

Cosmo tested his helmet's communicator. "Nuri, Brain-E, can you hear me?" he said into its microphone.

He heard the hiss of static, then Nuri's voice reply in his earpiece. "Receiving you loud and clear."

Cosmo heard a bleep. "This is Brain-E, Master Cosmo. We're right behind you."

Their voices sounded strange in his helmet; tinny and echoing under the water. It felt like he was in a bubble, his helmet amplifying the hum of the ocean. "Nuri, can you check our bearings, please?"

Nuri glided alongside him, checking

her compass. "Calzador is due east," she replied. "Follow me."

"Brain-E, keep your sensors on full alert for Hydronix," Cosmo said as they headed towards Calzador.

Cosmo could see shafts of sunlight streaking down through the water, lighting microscopic specks of gold. It was the golden plankton that Nuri had told him about earlier: the tiny organisms that gave the sea its golden colour. They glittered on Cosmo's visor and landed on the coral blooms, which closed around them like tiny mouths. Cosmo had never realized that coral was alive and needed to eat like any other creature.

"Brain-E, where does all this golden plankton come from?" he asked.

He heard a bleep in his earpiece. "The golden plankton on Oceania grows in a single warm mineral vent in the deepest part of the ocean. It drifts out on the current, providing nourishment for all sea life. This is why Oceania is home to so many underwater species."

Cosmo could see alien fish swimming among the corals. They were unlike any he'd seen back on Earth. He noticed a large flatfish that was walking on its fins, another fish hoovering up the sand with a long tube-like mouth, and a huge shoal of bright pink fish that swam together so that they looked like one big fish.

"Hey, what's that ahead of us?" Nuri said over the communicator. She was accelerating quickly. "Oh no, it's a sunken sightseeing submarine!"

Cosmo sped after her and saw the submarine lying on its side, its propeller still spinning. It was dented and battered, its portholes smashed and its cabin flooded. Cosmo's heart sank. "Hydronix must have done this," he said.

Nuri peered in through a porthole and

realized that the sub was deserted.
"What do you think happened to its
passengers?" she asked.

Brain-E bleeped. "I hate to think."

Out of the corner of his visor, Cosmo
noticed a ghostly fish-tailed alien
watching them from among the corals.
It looked like one of the creatures that

had helped him free Jako. He spoke quietly into his microphone: "Brain-E, are there such things as underwater ghosts on Oceania?"

Brain-E's lights flashed as it scanned its databank for information. "Do you mean merlocks, Master Cosmo? They're known as the 'spirits of the ocean', a shy alien species that live among the reefs and care for the underwater creatures here."

So I wasn't imagining things before, Cosmo thought. *It was merlocks that helped me save Jako.*

As he eyed the ghostly form, another thought popped into his head. "Nuri, I think the passengers probably made it out alive," he said.

"What makes you say that?" Nuri asked.

"Merlocks are here," Cosmo replied. *The merlocks wouldn't have let the passengers perish*, he realized.

"Look, there's one behind you."

As Nuri turned round, the merlock suddenly swam off through the ocean, beckoning as if it wanted them to follow. Cosmo and Nuri kicked their torpedo fins and sped through the water after it.

Nuri checked her compass. "It's taking us in the direction of Calzador," she said.

"Perhaps it's seen Hydronix," Cosmo replied, bracing himself for trouble.

The merlock swam fast, moving through the water like mist. It led them further and further eastwards, and it wasn't long before Cosmo saw the great coral city of Calzador. It was one of the most incredible places he had ever seen: an enormous mass of underwater coral structures connected by walkways and bridges. At the city's entrance stood huge coral gate towers, but the gates were hanging open, smashed off their hinges as if something had pushed its way through.

"It looks as though Hydronix has beaten us here," Nuri said. She took her phaser gun off her utility belt and held it at the ready as they followed the merlock through the broken gates.

Inside the city, broken coral floated and clattered against Cosmo's visor. He saw a huge honeycomb structure of houses, purple and yellow and red in colour. Many had huge cracks in them; some were smashed to smithereens. He saw merlocks peering fearfully from windows, and terrified alien fish darting through the water: squawking winged fish, flashing neon-yellow shrimps and purple-spotted rays.

The merlock that had led them into the city swam off to hide, but Cosmo carried on, looking around at the broken coral archways and toppled coral columns. He saw a blue-domed building with an enormous hole smashed through its side.

"Hydronix has torn this place apart," Cosmo said into his mic.

There was a bleep as Brain-E replied: "The poor merlocks. They built Calzador over ten thousand years ago. It's their home."

Cosmo felt angry seeing the destruction Hydronix had caused, and a brave power stirred inside him, causing his Quantum Mutation Suit to glow. "Where's Hydronix now?" he said angrily.

Cosmo was about to propel himself forward in pursuit of the invader when he felt Nuri's hand on his shoulder. She pointed through the hole in the domed building to a large fish with fearsome teeth that was swimming towards them. It was some kind of alien shark.

"Cosmo, I don't think Hydronix is our only problem right now," she said over the communicator. "That thing looks hungry. Brain-E, please identify."

The brainbot bleeped in distress. "Species: razor-jaw," it replied. "And I think it's looking for something to eat . . ."

The razor-jaw was swimming closer, its mouth open wide.

"It's found something," Nuri said. "Us!"

CHAPTER FOUR

"SWIM FOR IT!"

Cosmo, Nuri and Brain-E sped away from the razor-jaw.

"This way!" Cosmo called, diving into a garden of coral trees. He kicked his legs hard, zipping between pink coral palms. He glanced over his shoulder and saw the razor-jaw still coming after them. "In here," he said, hiding among a clump of swaying coral ferns.

Nuri and Brain-E squeezed in beside

him, keeping quiet and still.

Through a small gap, Cosmo saw the razor-jaw swim into the garden. Its head was swishing left and right, its nostrils sniffing the water. Cosmo could feel his heart pounding. He saw the razor-jaw swimming towards the ferns where they were hiding. It had picked up their scent.

Uh-oh! he thought. "Nuri, it's on to us," he whispered into his microphone. "I'm going to use the Quantum Mutation Suit and transform into something huge to scare it off."

"No, Cosmo. You need to save your power for Hydronix," Nuri replied. "I'll deal with this."

She switched her phaser gun to stun mode and swam out from the ferns. The razor-jaw came towards her, its mouth opening to reveal dagger-like teeth.

Nuri took aim, her finger on the trigger, ready to release a high-voltage stun, when

suddenly a merlock appeared at the
entrance to the garden and swam
quickly between her and the razor-jaw.

What's it doing? Cosmo wondered.

The merlock faced the awesome razor-jaw and raised its ghostly hand. The razor-jaw stopped abruptly and then, as if obeying an order, turned and swam away.

Cosmo had never seen anything like it. "That was incredible!" he said into his communicator. "How did the merlock do that?"

He heard Brain-E's robotic voice reply over his earpiece. "Merlocks can communicate with all the ocean's creatures," it explained. "They do not speak, but use thought waves. It's called telepathy."

Cosmo and Brain-E swam out to thank the merlock for saving them, and Nuri put away her phaser gun. The underwater alien looked at Cosmo with its ghostly fish eyes.

"Thank you," Cosmo said loudly, hoping the merlock would hear him through his visor.

The merlock's expression did not change.

"We're from G-Watch," Cosmo added. "We're searching for the invader. Can you tell us what happened here?"

The merlock didn't move its lips, but Cosmo heard its voice replying in his head. *It destroyed our homes, and the homes of many ocean creatures – that razor-jaw was just angry.* Cosmo realized that the merlock was communicating with him using telepathy.

"How extraordinary," Brain-E remarked over the communicator. The brainbot had picked up the merlock's thought waves too, and was recording their frequency in its databank.

So where's Hydronix now? Cosmo wondered.

The merlock could hear his thoughts too. *Follow me*, it communicated by telepathy, leading them across the ruined city and out through two more toppled gates. It swam over a stretch of shattered coral to where the ocean bed dropped away like an underwater cliff.

Cosmo, Nuri and Brain-E swam over its edge and looked down into what seemed like infinite darkness.

The merlock pointed down into the depths. *The monster went into the abyss . . .*

Cosmo was perplexed. *What's Hydronix after down there?* he wondered.

My people fear the monster has gone in search of the great vent, the merlock replied.

Cosmo noticed microscopic golden plankton drifting up from the darkness and remembered what Brain-E had told him earlier – that the plankton grew in a vent in the deepest part of the ocean. "Brain-E, did you say that all the sea creatures on Oceania depend on the golden plankton for their survival?"

"Affirmative," Brain-E replied.

Of course! Cosmo realized. He glanced at Nuri and spoke gravely into his communicator: "Hydronix has been

heading for the thermal vent all along
– he's going to cut off the supply of
golden plankton!"

Nuri's blue face turned pale with
concern. "But he'll kill the whole planet!"

"Brain-E, will you look up the vent's
coordinates?" Cosmo asked.

Brain-E bleeped in his earpiece.
"Master Cosmo, I'm afraid the exact
whereabouts of the vent are unrecorded.
It is so deep that it has not been
mapped."

But we have to get there fast, Cosmo
thought. He turned back to the
merlock for help, but it had already
read his mind.

Follow the call of the jumbola whales,
it told him. *They will lead you there.*

Cosmo nodded gratefully. *Thank you
again for saving us. Now it's our turn to
save you.*

The merlock smiled. *Good luck.*

"Come on, team. Let's go," Cosmo said into his mic. They waved goodbye to the merlock, then dived down, kicking their legs hard, their torpedo fins sending them deep into the abyss. "We've got to get to the vent before Hydronix!"

CHAPTER FIVE

THE EVIL PLAN

Meanwhile, far across the universe on the battleship *Oblivion*, the outlaw Kaos was seated at a long dining table, a spoon in each hand.

A small purple rat dragged a plate of food across the table and placed it in front of him.

Kaos's five heads stared at the food in disgust. It was the poached brain of a giant comet beetle.

"I'm sick to death of eating the dregs of the universe," one head said.

"Me too!" said another.

"And me!"

"And me!"

"And me!"

Reluctantly Kaos dipped his spoon into the brain and started feeding his five mouths, each one retching as it swallowed.

The purple rat squeaked nervously, looking up at its master.

"If you must know, Wugrat, it's disgusting!" one head said, spitting a mouthful of brain at the rat.

"The sooner we return to the galaxy the better," a second added. "The Doom Vortex has such revolting cuisine."

A third head grimaced. "When we take over the galaxy, we will hold a banquet to celebrate, offering the very finest delicacies."

"Such as?" a fourth asked.

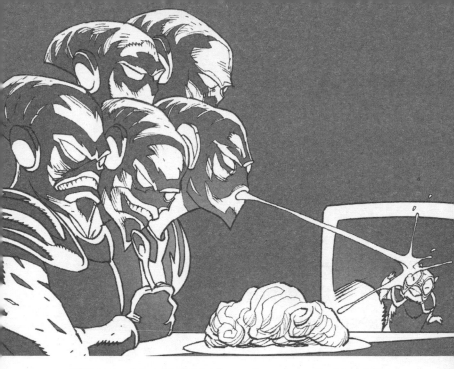

"How about G1's head on a platter?"

The other four heads roared with laughter. "Oh, what a treat!" they said.

The purple rat squeaked, scurrying back and forth anxiously.

"Oh, don't be such a worry-rat," the first head sneered. "Hydronix will soon finish off Oceania. And once that stupid planet's destroyed, there won't be any more holidays – only terror and fear all over the galaxy. Fear of me!"

"And me!"

"And me!"

"And me!"

"Me too!"

* * *

Back on Oceania, as the G-Watch agents descended into the abyss, Nuri kept track of the depth using a handheld echo-sounder. "Two hundred metres . . . three hundred metres . . . four hundred metres."

The light from the sun grew dimmer the deeper they swam, until there was no light at all. They were far down, swimming in total darkness.

Cosmo couldn't see anything. It was frightening, as if a lid had been put on top of the ocean. He unclipped a plasma torch from his utility belt and switched it on, lighting the way. Nuri did the same. Swimming by torchlight was eerie.

Strange-looking deep-sea creatures passed through the beams: a big white fish with no eyes sensing its way with antennae, a jellyfish the size of a hot-air balloon and a shoal of glowing green sea-apes. All the while, flecks of golden plankton swirled and sparkled in the torchlight.

Nuri spoke over the communicator: "I don't hear any jumbola whales calling."

Cosmo was listening too, but the pressure of the deep water was filling his helmet with a claustrophobic hum. He spoke into his microphone. "Brain-E, is anything coming up on your scanner?"

"Not yet, Master Cosmo. Jumbola whales should be here somewhere though. They breathe air on the surface, then dive down into the abyss to feed."

"Nuri, how deep can we go before our suits burst?" Cosmo asked.

Nuri shone her torch onto the echo-sounder that read the depth. Her reply

crackled in Cosmo's earpiece, the pressure affecting its signal. "G-Watch spacesuits can withstand three times this depth," she replied. "And the Quantum Mutation Suit can go even deeper."

Cosmo kicked his feet, powering himself down, hoping to hear the call of a jumbola whale that would lead them to the vent. Suddenly he felt something long and thick brush against his leg. He froze, thinking it might be a tentacle, but when he shone his torch on it, he saw that he was swimming through a white kelp forest. The long snake-like seaweed was growing on the side of an underwater mountain. Cosmo followed the slope down, speeding onwards with his torpedo fins.

In the torchlight he saw craggy peaks and jagged ridges jutting out around him. He gasped as two huge red eyes appeared, watching from a cave, but when he shone his torch inside, he saw that it was just a large striped lobster.

Brain-E bleeped in his earpiece. "I'm detecting vibrations in the water, Master Cosmo. Calling sounds like bells."

Cosmo and Nuri both stopped and listened.

"I can hear them too," Nuri said, her pointy Etrusian ears twitching.

Then Cosmo heard a sound like bells tinkling in the distance. It was the call of a jumbola whale. "Where's it coming from?" he asked.

"Scanning," Brain-E replied in Cosmo's earpiece.

Cosmo shone his torch all around, trying to locate the whale. He heard the brainbot bleep quickly, its lights flashing in distress.

"Master Cosmo, Miss Nuri, it's coming from directly above us!"

Cosmo glanced up, his torch illuminating what looked like a huge cave above them.

But it wasn't a cave. It was the open mouth of a jumbola whale diving to feed. It surged downwards, sweeping them up inside it.

"Whoa!" Cosmo yelled, tumbling over and over.

"Help!" Brain-E cried. "We're done for!"

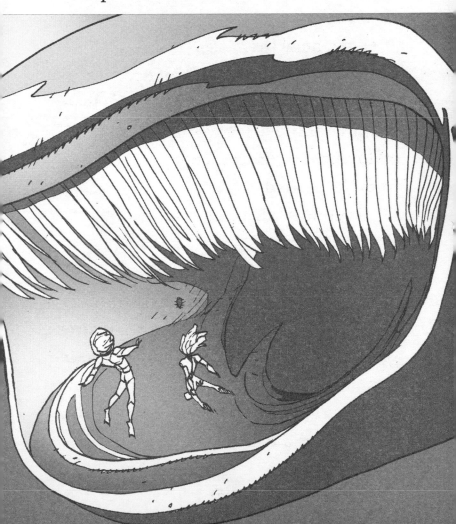

CHAPTER SIX

"HELP!"

Cosmo whirled round and round inside the jumbola whale's mouth, water and golden plankton swirling around him. By the light of his torch he could see Nuri holding onto its enormous tongue, trying to stop herself from being swallowed.

Brain-E was clasping onto her ankle. "Help!" the brainbot bleeped.

The whale's mouth closed and Cosmo felt the water surge forward, pushing him against a curtain of thick bristles. In his torchbeam he saw water gushing out through the bristles, leaving thick golden slime inside the whale's mouth. The huge tongue rose upwards and Nuri leaped off it, landing by Cosmo at the front of the mouth, as the whale tipped the plankton down its throat.

It's filter-feeding, Cosmo realized. He remembered from his lessons at school that whales ate plankton. "Don't worry – it doesn't want to eat us," he said into his mic. "It's not dangerous."

"I still think we'd be safer out of here," Nuri replied.

"No, hold on. The jumbola will be heading for the thermal vent where the plankton grows. We can get a ride."

They gripped the curtain of bristles as the whale opened its vast mouth again, letting in another surge of sparkling water. The water swirled around then was spewed back out through the bristles, leaving more plankton behind. As the jumbola swallowed, a rumble came from deep within its stomach and it belched, blasting Cosmo and Nuri with a warm salty wind. Cosmo held the bristles firmly every time the water surged, peering out to see where the jumbola was heading.

The whale was swimming down towards the very bottom of the abyss. In the distance Cosmo could make out a glow. It was plankton, a great golden cloud of it rising from a chasm in the deep ocean floor. *The thermal vent*, he realized. "Nuri, Brain-E, we're here!"

In the light from the vent Cosmo could see other whales swimming around it, feeding on the nutritious plankton. He heard their calls vibrating through the water.

All of a sudden a fierce bellow sounded, making Cosmo's whole body shudder.

The whales scattered, and the jumbola they were riding in veered quickly away.

"What was that sound?" Nuri asked.

In the pale golden light Cosmo saw movement on the mountainside: it was a fierce creature with enormous thrashing tentacles, purple scales, fins and webbed feet. Cosmo saw its menacing barnacled

face: frilled gills protruded like horns above its piercing red eyes.

"It's Hydronix!"

The invader tore a huge rocky overhang from the mountainside and hurled it into the thermal vent.

"He's trying to block the vent!" Nuri gasped.

"What are we going to do?" Brain-E asked nervously.

It's time to fight, Cosmo thought. He felt his power well up inside him and his spacesuit glowed. "I'm going out there!"

Nuri reached for his arm. "I've got an idea that might help," she said. "I'll follow you down in a moment."

Cosmo pushed through the jumbola's bristles and out of its mouth, leaving Nuri and Brain-E still inside. He kicked his torpedo fins and sped towards the alien invader. "In the name of G-Watch, I order you to stop!" he called.

Hydronix turned and saw Cosmo. "Get away, boy, or face the consequences!" he bellowed. He grabbed another huge lump of rock with his massive tentacles and threw it down into the vent.

It's time to use the Quantum Mutation Suit, Cosmo decided. With it, he could transform into a fearsome alien to fight the invader. He spoke into his helmet's sensor: "SCAN."

On the electronic visor in front of his eyes, images of alien creatures appeared as the suit scrolled through its databank: a toxic darmatrian, a spiny prokopax, a claw-toothed icegull. *What alien can beat something as powerful as Hydronix?* Cosmo wondered. He saw an image of a large underwater alien with pincers.

ALIEN: GAURON
SPECIES: GIGANTACRAB
ORIGIN: PLANET CRUX
HEIGHT: 5.4 METRES
WEIGHT: 4.1 TONNES
FEATURE: MASSIVE PINCERS

Massive pincers should hold him! Cosmo thought, and he spoke the command: "MUTATE!"

CHAPTER SEVEN

SQUEEZED TO A PASTE!

Cosmo's power surged through the
Quantum Mutation Suit, and he felt it
fusing with his skin. His body tingled
as every molecule inside him began to
transform. He was growing huge, his skin
mutating into a thick exoskeleton as hard
as rock, his neck forming gills so that he
could breathe underwater, and his eyes
poked out on stalks. His arms and legs
multiplied: six of them grew, each long and

articulated, then his hands changed into huge pincers. He was Gauron the gigantacrab, and he was ready to do battle!

Hydronix held another great chunk of rock aloft, ready to hurl it into the thermal vent. As Gauron, Cosmo felt strong.

"I wouldn't do thaaat if I were yooou!" he snapped, his voice sounding garbled underwater.

Hydronix turned in surprise. "Where did you come from?" he bellowed.

Without replying, Cosmo clamped his pincers onto the huge lump of rock, ripping it out of the invader's grasp and hurling it away from the vent.

Hydronix lashed at Cosmo with a mighty tentacle, but Cosmo grabbed hold of it with his huge claw. He hurled the invader off the underwater mountainside, sending him spinning through the ocean.

The alien bellowed with anger as he landed on the ocean floor. He rose up, bubbles gushing from his mouth. "Do not staaand in my waaaay!"

Cosmo snapped his mighty pincers. "Leave this planet, Hydronix!"

But the invader swam towards him and lashed out again, whipping his tentacles through the water, fleshy suckers along their length. "NEVER!"

All at once, the tentacles wrapped around Cosmo's mighty pincers, clamping them shut. Cosmo tugged, trying to pull himself free, but the invader closed in, coiling the tentacles round and round Cosmo's hard shell. Cosmo could feel them squeezing him. Hydronix's strength was awesome.

"I will squeeze you to a paste!" the alien bellowed.

Cosmo heard a loud *crack!* as his gigantacrab exoskeleton split. He was

being crushed! Air seeped out of his gills and he felt his power weakening. His stalk eyes bulged as if they were about to pop.

"RESET," he gasped. Instantly his body began shrinking and the tentacles around him loosened. He turned back into his boy self in the Quantum Mutation Suit, and quickly swam out of Hydronix's grasp.

"What trick is this?" the invader bubbled in surprise.

Cosmo took cover in a cave in the mountainside, trying to gather his strength. He saw an angry red eye peer in at him.

"I will destroooy this planet and yooou with it!" the invader roared. Hydronix tore a huge slab of rock from the mountainside and hurled it towards the vent. The rock went spinning through the water, then crashed down onto the vent like a giant lid. Immediately the thermal flow was cut off and the golden glow of plankton in the water began to fade.

"Hahahaha!" Hydronix bellowed. "There's nothing you caaan dooo now!"

I have to open that vent up again, Cosmo thought. *Or all the ocean life on the planet will die!*

"SCAN," he said into his helmet's sensor. On his visor, digital images of alien creatures flashed in front of his eyes: a spike-tailed genyaden, a five-fanged kalevon, a venomous slox. He paused on an image of a fish-like alien with a head the size of a demolition ball.

```
ALIEN: RAMROD
SPECIES: GRUPEROID
ORIGIN: PLANET ALUA
HEIGHT: 10.1 METRES
WEIGHT: 7.8 TONNES
FEATURE: INDESTRUCTIBLE SKULL
```

With an indestructible skull I could bust that rock too pieces – and Hydronix too! Cosmo thought. "MUTATE!"

CHAPTER EIGHT

A SHOCKING END

Cosmo tingled as the Quantum Mutation Suit activated, his molecules transforming once again. Shiny black scales began spreading over his skin. He grew larger, his arms turning into fins and his legs fusing into a powerful tail. His skull thickened into the massive skull of Ramrod. It was the size of a demolition ball and made of solid bone.

Cosmo swished his tail, speeding like

a battering ram towards the rock that
was blocking the vent. He hit it headfirst,
smashing it apart. Hot bubbling water
gushed out of the vent, sending pieces of
rock flying. Plankton shone like gold,
whooshing into the ocean once more.

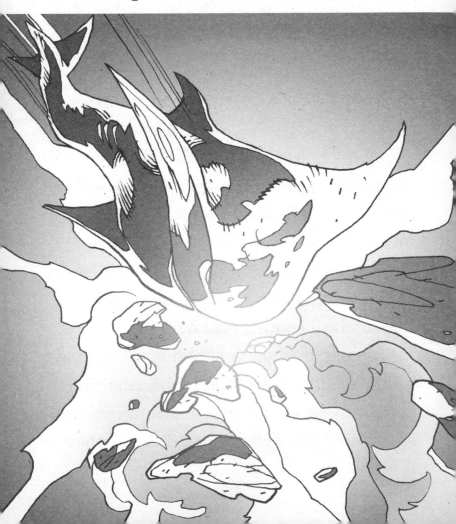

"You fool!" Hydronix bellowed. He quickly shot his strong tentacles around Cosmo and slammed him into the vent, holding him down so that hot water bubbled beneath Cosmo's gruperoid body. "I'll use you to plug the vent instead!"

Cosmo struggled but he was held too tightly. His scales were steaming. He was beginning to cook. *I don't fancy turning into alien seafood!* he thought, his power failing. "RESET!" he said.

Cosmo felt himself shrink as he turned back into his boy self. He tried to swim away, but Hydronix grabbed hold of him again. "Not so fast, boy," the invader bellowed. He pushed Cosmo back down into the hot vent. "I will destroy you and everything else here too!"

Boiling water was bubbling all around Cosmo, and the Quantum Mutation Suit was heating up. Golden plankton swirled in front of his visor. He reached for the

vent's rim, trying to pull himself out, but Hydronix pushed him deeper. *I've met my match this time*, he thought desperately.

Just then, a voice came over his earpiece. "Hold on, Cosmo, we're on our way." It was Nuri! He glanced up and saw her riding towards the vent on the back of the jumbola whale, with Brain-E beside her. "Let him go, Hydronix!" he heard her say.

The jumbola powered towards the invader. It banked, swishing its massive tail, knocking the invader to the ocean floor. Cosmo felt the alien's grip loosen around him. He kicked hard and swam free of the vent. "Thanks, Nuri," he said into his mic.

But Hydronix wasn't finished yet. The invader rose up and shot out a tentacle, grabbing the jumbola and swinging it through the water. Nuri and Brain-E tumbled off its back, rolling over and over as the jumbola spun away. The invader shot out another tentacle towards Nuri, and she blasted it with her phaser gun.

"That thing doesn't hurt me!" Hydronix bellowed. He struck her, sending her crashing to the sea bed.

Quickly Brain-E propelled itself towards Hydronix and jabbed the invader in the eye with its metal probe arm. "Take that!"

Hydronix roared angrily and swept the brainbot away as if it was a shrimp.

"Hey, leave them alone! They're my friends!" Cosmo yelled. *I have to do something*, he thought. *And quickly.*

"SCAN," he said into his helmet's sensor.

On its visor, images of more aliens appeared. *What is a match for Hydronix?* he wondered. He saw an image of a sparking sea serpent and had an idea.

ALIEN: ELECTRAX
SPECIES: PULSE-SERPENT
ORIGIN: PLANET REET
LENGTH: 6.6 METRES
WEIGHT: 1.3 TONNES
FEATURES: ELECTRIC SHOCKS

Electric shocks could come in handy! "MUTATE!" he said.

Immediately he began to transform into the pulse-serpent. His arms and legs receded into his body and he started to lengthen. He grew long and eel-like, and a tingle of electricity ran up and down his flexible spine. He weaved through the water towards Hydronix.

"Sssstop," Cosmo hissed, flicking a forked tongue from his serpent mouth.

Hydronix faced him. "And what are you going to do about it, worm?" he roared, lashing out with his tentacles, trying to coil them around Cosmo's serpent body.

"Cosmo! What are you doing? He'll crush you!" Nuri yelled.

But as Electrax, Cosmo wove among Hydronix's tentacles, brushing his long flexible body against their suckers. "I've ssssome shocking news for you, Hydronix!" he hissed, and in a flash, electricity pulsed from him.

"Aarrgghh!" Hydronix bellowed, his tentacles sparking from the shock. Cosmo let out another pulse of electricity, and the invader lit up like a neon bulb.

"Noooo!" Hydronix roared. He shuddered violently, his tentacles twitching.

Cosmo wrapped around him, sending high-voltage electricity through the invader, turning his tentacles limp.

"What have you done to me?" Hydronix bellowed.

"RESET!" Cosmo said, and instantly

his serpent body shrank as he turned back into a boy again.

The invader looked at Cosmo with an expression of sheer hatred, his tentacles hanging limp by his sides. "I will not be beaten!"

"You've caused enough destruction here, Hydronix," Cosmo said. He felt his power welling up inside him again, and the mutation suit glowed more brightly. He felt his arm and then his hand tingle as a sword of light began to extend from it like a bolt of lightning. It was the power sword, the physical form of the power inside him. "Let's see how you handle the power of the universe!" he said. He surged towards the alien and plunged the sword into him.

Hydronix screamed, and for a moment their wills were locked in battle, their very molecules fighting one another. Cosmo could feel his power grappling with Hydronix's destructive rage. The invader writhed and bellowed: "Aarrgh!" His barnacled body squirmed, his fins rippled and his purple suckered flesh began to blister. He was shrivelling, his tentacles flapping like weed; then, with a last cry, he exploded in a cloud of bubbles.

CHAPTER NINE

BEATEN!

"You've done it! You've defeated Hydronix!" Cosmo heard Nuri say in his earpiece. She swam to his side, and held him in the water as he floated, exhausted, at the edge of the thermal vent, golden plankton billowing around him. "Well done, Cosmo!"

Brain-E scuttled along the ocean floor, its propeller bent and broken. "Master Cosmo, Electrax was a very clever transformation indeed."

Cosmo smiled, relieved that the invader had been defeated. Through the hum of the ocean he heard a sound like chiming bells. He looked up and saw the jumbola whale circling overhead, with more following it, returning to feed on the plankton.

"Nuri, how did you manage to get the jumbola to help you?" Cosmo asked her. "It saved my life, whacking Hydronix away like that."

"I couldn't have done it without Brain-E," Nuri replied. "He had stored the frequency for the thought-wave telepathy used by the merlocks. He used it to explain to the jumbola that you were in trouble. It was only too pleased to assist."

"Neat trick," Cosmo said.

Brain-E bleeped proudly.

"We should get back to the Dragster and tell G1 the good news," Nuri said.

Cosmo glanced at the thermal vent and smiled. "Oceania's safe again. We did it."

Brain-E's lights flashed excitedly. "Full speed to the surface!"

Together they pushed off from the bottom of the ocean and zoomed up through the golden water.

Aboard the battleship *Oblivion*, Kaos was writhing on the floor clutching his stomach. "I knew we shouldn't have eaten that beetle brain," one of his heads said, wincing. "I feel sick!"

Wugrat entered the room, squeaking anxiously.

"What's the matter now, Wugrat, you useless ball of fur?"

The purple rat nibbled its whiskers then squeaked again.

"What's that you say? Hydronix's navicom signal has vanished?"

Kaos pulled himself over to a console in the corner of the room and pressed a series of buttons. "This can't be happening," one head said.

The console's monitor was blank.

"Perhaps the machine's faulty," another head suggested.

Kaos gave the monitor a thump. "It's

not faulty. Hydronix has failed!"

"Blasted G-Watch!" the heads all spat.

Kaos thumped the console in anger. "I won't stand for this. We will not be beaten! Wugrat, fetch another navicom."

The rat squeaked, then scampered away.

Kaos's heads looked at one another,

fuming, sick dripping from their chins. "We shall send in Atomic!"

"Yes, they'll be no match for Atomic!"

"Atomic! Atomic! Atomic!"

Still clutching his stomach, Kaos dragged himself through the corridors of the battleship to the cargo hold, where a single invader was standing ready for action, huge and steaming, his body glowing green.

The purple rat scurried in with a crystal disc in its mouth – a navicom transporter device. Kaos snatched it, turned its outer ring to set its coordinates, then attached it to the invader. "It is time, Atomic," he said.

"I will not fail you, Master," the mighty alien replied.

The navicom unit began flashing as the alien invader stepped to the centre of the cargo hold. The roof of the battleship *Oblivion* slid open to reveal the swirling

stars of the Doom Vortex. The light from
the navicom spread over Atomic's huge
green body; then, with a whoosh, he shot
out into space.

CHAPTER TEN

A WARM SEND-OFF

By the time Cosmo and Nuri reached
the ocean's surface, dusk was falling.
A golden evening glow radiated from
the water. Cosmo raised his visor and
breathed in the fresh salty air. "Oh, that
feels good," he said.

Brain-E bleeped. "What an underwater
adventure that was. It's a wonder my
circuits survived."

The Dragster 7000 was still bobbing

on the water where they had left it, beside
the remains of the broken holiday island.

As Cosmo pulled himself up onto its
floats, he heard voices in his mind:
Thank you . . . Thank you . . . Thank you . . .
He turned and saw merlocks swimming
to the surface to wave farewell.

He waved back, then opened the

Dragster's door and climbed aboard to prepare for takeoff.

Nuri and Brain-E followed him into the cockpit and the little brainbot shook its metal legs to dry off.

Nuri switched on the communications console, and the face of G1, the Chief of G-Watch appeared on the monitor.

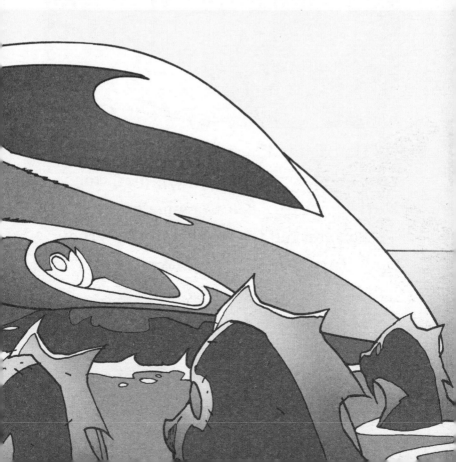

"Hydronix is defeated, G1," Nuri said.

G1's silver eyes glinted as he smiled. "Well done," he replied. "I knew I could count on you all."

"He tried to block Oceania's thermal vent and starve the ocean of plankton," Nuri explained. "But Cosmo stopped him."

"You can tell the holidaymakers they can return now, G1," Cosmo added. "The holiday season is back on."

"The galaxy is for ever in your debt, Cosmo," G1 said. "Thank you."

"I couldn't have done it without Nuri

and Brain-E," Cosmo told the Chief. He felt a warm feeling of friendship as he smiled at his team.

"Listen up, all three of you. Your mission is not over yet," G1 said. "G-Watch scanners have detected a fifth invader beaming into the galaxy. We believe it to be the last of them — Atomic, the radioactive bomb. Scanners calculate that he's heading for the mining planet Abu, where the galaxy's hyperdrive cells are made."

"We're onto it, Chief," Cosmo replied, starting the Dragster's thrusters.

"I must warn you that you'll need every ounce of skill and strength at your disposal," G1 added. "Atomic will be the most powerful invader you've faced yet. Good luck. The end is in sight."

The screen flickered as the transmission ended.

Cosmo checked the controls for takeoff,

then turned to Nuri. "When all this is over, I think we deserve a holiday," he said.

"If we're still alive," Nuri replied anxiously. "You just heard what G1 said."

Cosmo pulled back the throttle and the thrusters roared, lifting the Dragster 7000 off the water and blasting it up through the mauve sky. He looked down at

the peaceful ocean, relieved that Oceania was saved. "Set a course for Planet Abu, Nuri. It's four down, one to go!"

But as they sped up through the planet's atmosphere, off to fight the final invader, Cosmo couldn't get G1's daunting words out of his mind: *Atomic will be the most powerful invader you've faced yet.*

Join Cosmo on his next **ALIEN INVADERS**
mission. He must face – and defeat

ATOMIC
THE RADIOACTIVE BOMB

INVADER ALERT!

On the mining planet Abu, quarry worker
Gooka Bik powered up a drillatron machine.
Its photon battery hummed and the
machine's headlights lit up a glowing green
mist as Gooka pumped his legs, moving its
piston stilts across the stony ground. The
drillatron lurched forward like a hulking
robot, its glass-bubble cab encasing Gooka,
protecting him from Planet Abu's toxic air.

Gooka was starting his shift in Abu's
quarry six, mining for radonium ore – the
most precious mineral in the galaxy. He
guided the drillatron to the rockface, where
a truck was waiting, then squeezed two
triggers in its claw arms, gripping the rock
with the machine's metal claws. He switched
on its enormous iron drill and pressed it
into the rockface. Rockdust shot out over
his cab as the drill extracted large chunks
of luminous green radonium ore.

Gooka lowered the drillatron's scooper,
shovelling up the mineral-rich rock, then
turned the machine and tipped the load
onto the back of the waiting truck.

He worked for three solid Abu hours,

drilling the rockface until the truck was fully loaded. "You're good to go," he radioed to the truck's android driver.

"Affirmative," came the driver's reply.

Gooka wiped sweat from his hairy face as the fully-laden truck trundled down the quarry side heading for the planet's nuclear reactor. There, the radonium ore would be processed into hyperdrive cells to be used in spaceships for hyperspeed space travel.

Gooka worked for the Galactron Fuel Corporation. For half of each lunar month he would leave his family on Planet Vega and come to work on Abu. He knew the risks like all quarry workers did: exposure to the planet's toxic air could lead to radiation sickness, causing madness and even death, but the pay was high, and he was skilled at his job.

Gooka watched from his glass cab as the truck vanished into the mist, trundling onto Abu's mudflats and swamplands. He glanced to the sky, thinking of his family on Planet Vega. *Just a half-moon more and I'll be home to see you*, he thought.

A light flickered overhead and Gooka heard a distant rumble like thunder.

Strange, no elecro-magnetic storms forecast, he thought. The rumble grew louder, then he gasped as he saw a large object powering down from above. It slammed into the base of the quarry, and in a mighty explosion the drillatron was hurled against the rockface, its glass-bubble cab shattering.

Whoop! Whoop! Its alarm sounded, signalling that toxic air was getting in.

Gooka radioed for help: "This is Gooka Bik. Something just smashed down into quarry six. My cab's broken. Help, I'm breathing radonium gas!" His throat was tightening and he coughed.

The voice of the quarry manager Florian Dax replied from base. "Stay calm. We're coming to get you."

Still coughing, Gooka glanced back and gasped in horror. From a crater in the ground an enormous alien was rising. *I must be hallucinating*, Gooka thought, dizzy from the toxic air. He rubbed his eyes in disbelief, but the creature was now coming towards him! It towered taller than the drillatron, glowing toxic green and steaming. It roared: "I am Atomic, and I am here on the orders of Kaos to blow this planet up!"

CHAPTER ONE
A LONG WAY FROM EARTH

"Set a course for Planet Abu, Agent Nuri," Cosmo said.

Agent Nuri, Cosmo's blue-skinned Etrusian co-pilot, inputted the flight data into the spaceship's navigation console. "Checking available routes now," she replied.

Cosmo felt nervous but excited. He was off on the final leg of his mission for the galactic security force G-Watch, flying the Dragster 7000 spaceship away from Planet Oceania towards the galaxy's Outer Rim.

"Done," Nuri said. She tapped the spacescreen, activating its star plotter, and words lit up on its glass:

DESTINATION: PLANET ABU
STAR SYSTEM: OUTER RIM
ROUTE: HYPERWAY 7 FROM SIRIUS
DISTANCE: 1.7 BILLION MILES

Cosmo turned the Dragster towards Sirius, a red star marked on the spacescreen. He powered the Dragster at eleven vectrons, and the cockpit filled with red starlight.

Brain-E, the ship's brainbot, bleeped from the control desk. "Steer clear of its solar flares, Master."

Cosmo had only ever seen Sirius through a telescope before – from Earth. Up close now, he saw massive explosions erupting from its surface, sending out burning solar flares. "Thanks for the warning, Brain-E," he said, nudging the steering column and giving the red star a wide berth.

"Good teamwork," Nuri smiled.

Cosmo felt glad that Nuri and Brain-E were with him. He piloted the Dragster round Sirius then zipped between a line of space beacons onto Hyperway Seven, one of the galaxy's major space lanes. "Engaging hyperdrive now," Cosmo said, flicking a switch on the steering column. The stars turned to bright white streaks and he was thrust back into his seat as the Dragster blasted across the galaxy at hyperspeed.

Cosmo's mission was to defeat five alien invaders that had been beamed into the galaxy by the outlaw Kaos, each with orders to destroy. So far he had defeated four of them: Rockhead, the living mountain; Infernox, the firestarter; Zillah, the fanged predator; and Hydronix, destroyer of the deep. Now he was flying to Planet Abu in the galaxy's Outer Rim to face the last of the invaders: the radioactive alien Atomic.

"Prepare to exit hyperdrive on my count," Nuri said. *"Three . . . two . . . one . . . now!"*

Cosmo flicked the hyperdrive switch back and adjusted course, his ears popping as the Dragster veered off the hyperway and slowed to eight vectrons.

As the stars reappeared in the spacescreen, he stared out excitedly. *This is the furthest I've ever been from Planet Earth,* he thought. He saw docking pods where huge space-cranes were loading containers onto star freighters, and a string of floating industrial platforms stretching into the distance. "What is this place?" he asked.

Nuri tapped the spacescreen and words flashed on its glass, naming the astral objects: SUB-STATION ENERGAX . . . DEPOT 5 . . . GALACTRON HYPERWORKS . . .

Brain-E bleeped. "The galaxy's Outer Rim is managed by the Galactron Fuel Corporation," it explained. "Hyperdrive cells for all the galaxy's spaceships are manufactured in space factories here, then taken to Planet Abu to be energized in its radonium reactor."

Planet Abu – that's where Kaos has beamed Atomic, Cosmo realized, and he gulped nervously seeing the planet marked on the star plotter: a remote planet of black rock with a haze of green light around it. "With the invader attacking Abu, all hyperdrive capability in the galaxy could now be under threat," Cosmo said. "Hold tight. I'm taking us in."

Cosmo sped towards Abu, slicing through the planet's atmosphere, then switched to planetary mode as the Dragster roared across its sky.

Abu's sky was dark – the only light coming from a glowing green mist below. Cosmo turned on the Dragster's searchlights and started to descend. Through the mist he saw the planet's surface dotted with barren hilltops. It looked like a harsh, desolate place. "Who'd want to live on a planet like this?" he wondered aloud.

"No one," Nuri replied. "Workers come here from other planets, but no one lives on Abu permanently. It's too dangerous."

A light flashed on the Dragster's external gauges:

ATMOSPHERIC WARNING: RADIOACTIVE

Brain-E bleeped. "Radonium is mined here, the most radioactive substance in the galaxy," the brainbot said. "Even the air here is toxic."

In the beam from the Dragster's searchlights, Cosmo saw mining machines working in quarries on the hillsides, and green mist swirling up from the rock.

"The mist is radonium gas," Brain-E continued. "If breathed in, radiation sickness will ensue, causing madness, then death."

Nuri checked the navigation console. "G-Watch's scanners calculated that the alien would have beamed in due east of here. Take us lower, Cosmo."

Cosmo pointed the Dragster eastwards and dived through the mist, wondering what sort of alien invader could survive in such a place. "Brain-E, what data do you have on Atomic?" he asked.

The brainbot's lights flashed. "Atomic originates from a radioactive star in the Doom Vortex, Master. He feeds on radiation and can detonate himself like a living bomb, exploding then reforming again and again."

"A radioactive living bomb!" Cosmo exclaimed, startled. Then he remembered the warning that G1, the chief of G-Watch, had given him when he had set off for Planet Abu: *Atomic will be the most powerful enemy you've faced.*

Cosmo gathered his courage and his spacesuit started to glow. As the Dragster cut through the swirling mist, flying close to the ground, he kept watch for the invader. He noticed a hillside quarry with a huge crater in it. "Nuri, what's that?" he asked, slowing and hovering above it.

Nuri peered down. "An impact crater!" she said. "Atomic must have beamed in *here*. Take us in to land, Cosmo."

Cosmo began his descent through the mist. But as he did, the Dragster's searchlights shone on a robot-like machine clawing frantically at the air. "That machine's going berserk. Something's wrong with it!" he said.

"It's a drillatron. Oh no, its cab's smashed!" Nuri replied.

Suddenly the machine jerked round and lunged for the Dragster, grabbing hold of it with a metal claw. *CLANG!*

"Hey, what's it doing?" Cosmo yelled.

The drillatron reached up with a second claw and clamped hold again. *CLUNK!*

"Whoa!" Cosmo struggled with the steering column as the Dragster lurched from side to side. He touched the thrusters, trying to shake the machine off, but it wasn't letting go.

"Its operator must be breathing toxic gas!" exclaimed Nuri. "He's got radiation sickness. He's going crazy!"

"Then we have to get to him, Nuri, and fix what's wrong with him before he shakes us to pieces."

Find out what happens in
ATOMIC – THE RADIOACTIVE BOMB . . .